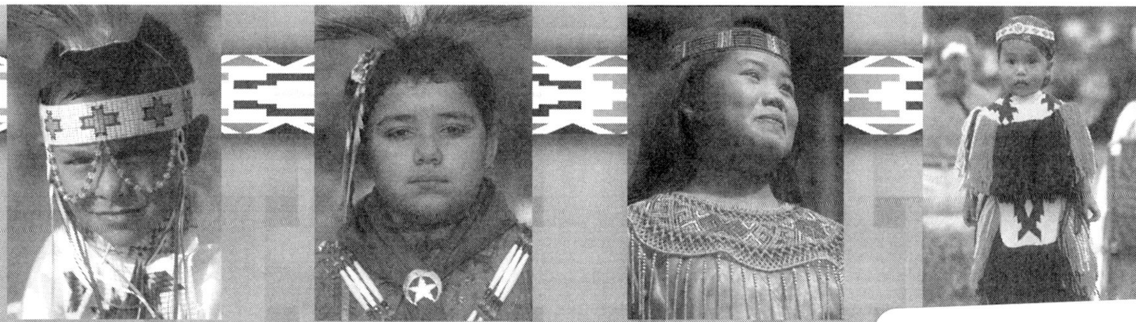

Indiana Native Americans

A Kid's Look at Our State's Chiefs, Tribes, Reservations, Powwows, Lore, and More From The Past and the Present

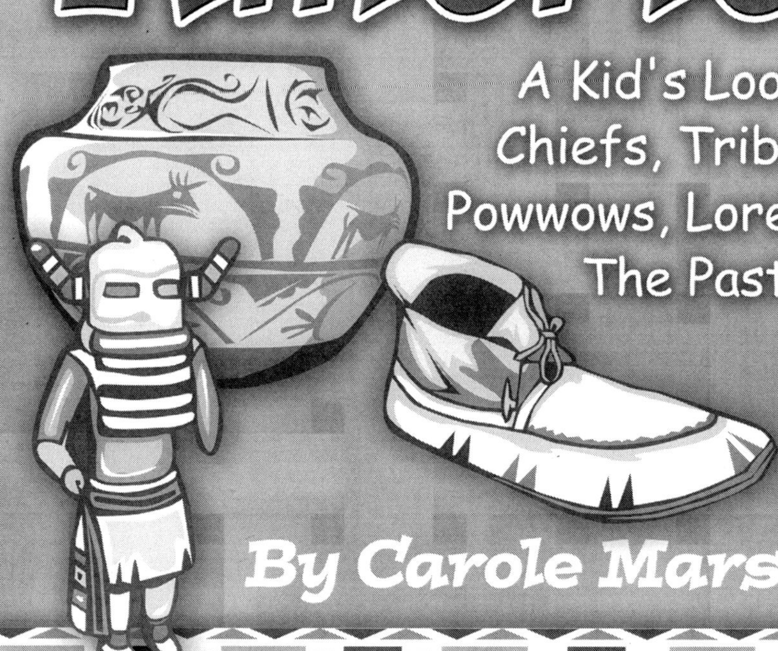

By Carole Marsh

Graphic Design: Lynette Rowe • Cover Design: Victoria DeJoy

NATIVE AMERICAN HERITAGE™

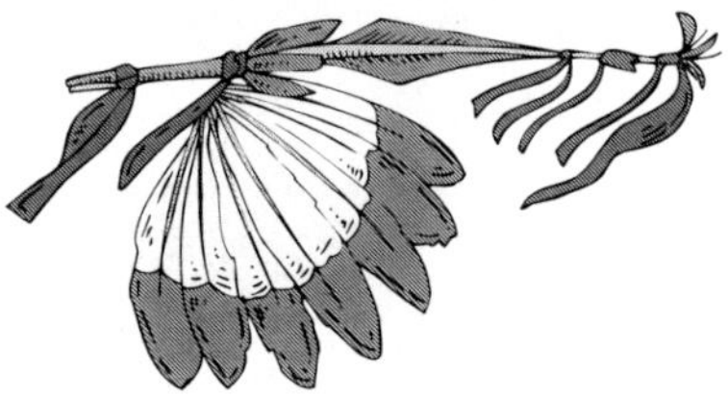

CAROLE MARSH BOOKS

Published by
GALLOPADE™ INTERNATIONAL
800-536-2GET
www.gallopade.com

Gallopade is proud to be a member of these educational organizations and associations:

The National School Supply and Equipment Association (NSSEA)
American Booksellers Association (ABA)
Virginia Educational Media Association (VEMA)
Association of Partners for Public Lands (APPL)
Museum Store Association (MSA)
National Association for Gifted Children (NAGC)
Publishers Marketing Association (PMA)
International Reading Association (IRA)
Association of African American Museums (AAAM)

Native American Heritage™ Series

Native American
Big Activity Book

Native American
Biographies

Native American
Coloring Book

Native American
Heritage Book

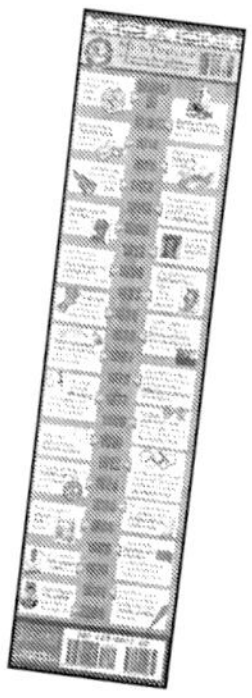
Native American
Timeline

Indiana State Stuff™

My First Pocket Guide: Indiana
My First Book About Indiana
Indiana Coloring Book
The Big Indiana Reproducible Activity Book
Jeopardy: Answers & Questions About Our State
Indiana "Jography!": A Fun Run Through Our State
Indiana Gamebooks
Indiana Bingo Games
Indiana Illustrated Timelines
Indiana Project Books
Indiana Bulletin Board Set
Indiana PosterMap
Indiana Stickers
Let's Discover Indiana! CD-ROM

Word from the Author

Hello!

I hope you are as interested in North America's wonderful Indian heritage as I am!

Like most kids, I grew up thinking of Indians as the other half of Cowboys. Today, of course, we are getting a much clearer and more accurate picture of what the first peoples on our land were all about. These "facts" are much more fascinating than anything Hollywood can make up. And you probably won't find much of this information in your history textbook!

I am 1/16 Cherokee. This is something I am very proud of and happy about. My grandmother was 1/4 Cherokee. She had tan skin, long gray hair and a very Indian look – especially if I did something bad! Her maiden name was Carrie Corn. Of course, when she got married, she took her husband's name, so it was many years before I learned to appreciate the significance of my native heritage.

Today, I'm trying to make up for lost time by exploring my roots as deeply as I can. One of the most interesting things I've learned is how fascinating all of the Indian tribes are – in the past, the present and future!

As you read about "your" Indians, remember that all native peoples were part of an ever-changing network of time, ideas, power and luck — good and bad. This is certainly a history that is not "dead," but continues to change – often right outside our own back doors! – all the time.

Carole Marsh
She-Who-Writes

PS: Many references show different spellings for the same word. I have tried to select the most common spelling for the time period described. I would not want to be in an Indian spelling bee!

A is for . . .

Awl

An Indian's "needle." Often made from wood, thorns, bone, or metal, it was used to punch holes in skins so they could be sewn together.

Adze

An Indian woodworking tool used to cut, scrape, or gouge; often used to hollow dugout canoes. Blades were made of stone, shell, bone or copper.

Angel Mounds State Historic Site

Evansville. Archaeologists estimate that these 11 mounds were the center of a village where 3,000 early Indians once lived. This was a large palisaded settlement on the Ohio River occupied from A.D. 1200 to 1450. Inhabitants were of the Mississippian culture. One mound is 44 feet high; another 4 acres in area. Built in the form of truncated pyramids. Not used for burials, but as the base of important buildings. The mile-long stockade was built in wattle and daub and made of 4,500 vertical logs. Here you can see replicas of an Indian dwelling, meetinghouse and temple.

American Indian Studies Research Institute

Indiana University, Bloomington.

Altar

A platform made of rocks or animal skulls; some had bowls, feathers, rattles, or skins on them. Indians prayed at these altars for things like good crops or expert hunting skills.

Arrow

A long, slender shaft made of reed, cane, or wood; pointed tip was attached to one end and split feathers to the other. Feathers helped the arrows fly straight.

Arts and Crafts

Early Indiana Indians made beautifully decorated pottery, finely carved stone figures of animals and human beings and sparkling jewelry.

Aborigine

A member of the earliest known population of a region.

Arrowhead

The pointed tip of an arrow, made of bone, antler, wood, or iron. Some tips had barbs that would embed themselves in flesh. These barbs made it difficult for an enemy to remove the arrowhead from a wound.

B is for . . .

Battle of Fallen Timbers

Where the Miami and other tribes were defeated by the Americans. After this, the British encouraged Great Lakes Indians to attack American settlements in the Northwest Territory.

Band

A subdivision of an Indian tribe. In earlier times, a band was sometimes created when part of a tribe split off from the main group. The band also chose new leadership.

Blankets

Used for door covers, partitions, bags, to dry food on, carry babies and many other purposes.

Baskets

Some were woven and others were coiled. Baskets were made from roots, grasses, barks, and other natural materials.

"Bury the Hatchet"

Expression that came into being when Chief Pontiac ended his war against the British at Fort Ouiatenon. He flung his tomahawk to the ground, indicating his willingness to stop fighting and start negotiating peace.

Battle of Tippecanoe

November, 1811; fought just north of Lafayette. Indians charged the American camp with so much courage that the troops at first fell back. But the American's firepower cut down the attackers. This defeat ended Shawnee Chief Tecumseh's dream to unite all Indian tribes to resist the expansion of whites into their lands.

Bow

Made from wood, horn or bone. Indiana Indian children learned how to use bows. The bowstring was made from animal gut, rawhide or twisted vegetable fibers.

Bone

Animal bones were used by Indiana Indians to make buttons, whistles and other items.

Beads

Made of wood, shells, claws, minerals, seeds — you name it! Later, the Indiana Indians traded with white men for glass beads, used in some of their decorative arts.

C is for . . .

Chief

Leader of a tribe. Different titles meant different things. Some members were made chief because they owned deeds to land. Chieftainship was often inherited, usually from the mother!

Contact Period

What historians call the era in the 1500s when Native Americans first met Europeans. This meeting changed the lifestyle of the Indiana Indians more than anyone could ever have anticipated!

Chief Pontiac

Brilliant Ottawa leader. In 1763, led an uprising of Great Lakes Indians against British rule. He peacefully took Fort Ouiatenon, but two years later, returned to the fort and ended his war in negotiation.

Calendar

Time was kept with notched sticks, knotted strings or a picture record. Days were divided into sunrise, noon, sunset and midnight. A full day was called a "night." Months were called "moons." Most Indians called a year a "winter."

Confederacy

A union of different groups of people. A confederacy in Indian culture was a group of tribes that agreed not to fight with each other. They agreed to live peacefully. Sometimes the tribes shared culture and language.

Chechawkose

Potawatomi chief who lived on the Tippecanoe River.

Citizenship

The Indian Citizenship Act of 1924 states all Indians born in the United States are citizens of the United States, and citizens of the states they live in, even though they may live on a reservation. They can vote. They pay most local, state and federal taxes, including sales taxes.

Clan

A tribal unit. Members are descended from the same ancestor.

Calumet

Also called "peace pipe" or "war pipe." Refers to the stem of the pipe, which is decorated with feathers or carved to signal the tribe's intentions. Believed to have great power.

Council Oak

Tree in Highland Cemetery at South Bend that is believed to be the site of a meeting between La Salle and tribal chiefs more than 300 years ago!

D is for . . .

Descendants

The first Indiana Indians were descendants of primitive hunters who crossed the Bering Strait from Asia to what is now Alaska. At that time, glacial ice still covered most of North America. These people were the true discoverers of the "New World!"

Dance

There were Indian dances for every occasion: war, peace, hunting, rain, good harvests, etc. Drums, rattles, and flutes of bone or reed provided the music. Dancers often chanted or sang while performing. Steps were not easy to learn and required consistent practice.

Disease

Indiana Indians had no immunity to the diseases that white explorers, colonists and settlers brought to their lands. These diseases included smallpox, measles, tuberculosis and others, which ravaged the tribes in great epidemics that killed many, and sometimes all, members of a tribe.

Did You Know You Could Go?

To these Indiana Indian events: Annual First Nations Pow Wow March, Bloomington; Annual Redbud Trail Rendezvous – April, Rochester; Annual IIM Pow Wow – May, Clearsprings; Annual United Metis Intertribal Gathering – June, Black Swan Lake; Annual White Buffalo Society Pow Wow – July, Gaston; Annual Gathering of the People Powwow – September, Terre Haute; Rochester; Annual Gourd Dance & Social – November, Clermont.

Dyes

Made of lichens, berries, roots, bark, plants, and other natural materials by Indians in Indiana. Different colors were used depending on what materials were available and what objects were to be dyed.

Dishes

Made from clay, bark, wood, stone, and other materials, depending on what was available and what food they would be used for.

Delaware Indians

Tribe also called the Lenni Lenape; came to Indiana to flee the domination of the Iroquois—the most important Algonquian confederacy. The English called them Delawares from their river.

Dreams

Important in the Indian tradition. It was believed that dreams were the "windows" to the soul. Many thought a person's hidden desires were expressed in dreams.

E is for . . .

Eagle

An animal used in many Indian ceremonies. Eagle feathers attached to war bonnets and shields communicated an Indian's rank in his tribe and what kinds of deeds he had done. Feathers also adorned rattles, pipes, baskets, and prayer sticks.

Eiteljorg Museum of American Indians and Western Art

Indianapolis; paintings, sculpture and more from the 19th century to the present, including the collection of the Museum of Indian Heritage.

Early Artisans

Ancient Great Lakes artisans learned how to hammer copper into axheads and spear points. They often found copper lying in chunks on the ground. By trial and error, they learned how to remove raw copper from inside certain rocks.

Earrings

Medicine men sometimes pierced male and female ears at special ceremonies. Earrings, which cost parents or relatives a significant amount, symbolized wealth and distinction. The more earrings that an Indian wore, the greater his honor. Some earrings measured 12 inches in length!

Environment

Preserving the environment is important to preserving Native American heritage. For thousands of years, Native American tribes lived completely off the land. Farming, mining, pollution have all had a part in changing native environments.

Eel River Indians

Part of the Miami who once lived in Boone County, Indiana.

English

In the 1800s, the U.S. government built boarding schools for Indian children throughout the nation. Children were forced to leave their homes and families to live at these schools. They were required to learn English and not speak their native languages.

Epidemics

Few Indians possessed immunity to the deadly diseases, like smallpox and measles, which European explorers and settlers brought to the New World. As a result, great population loss took place. Sometimes entire tribes became extinct. Epidemics sparked by Hernando De Soto's expedition are estimated to have killed 75% of the native population in the New World.

F is for . . .

Fetish

These small objects were thought to hold the spirit of an animal or a part of nature. A fetish could be an object found in nature, such as bone or wood, or it could be a carved object. The fetish was usually small enough to be carried in a small bag or on a cord. The making and use of a fetish was kept secret by its owner and only shared with the one who inherited it.

Fort Miami

One of the Indiana forts which fell to the Indians during the French and Indian War.

French and Indian War

Broke out in 1745 over boundary lines between New France and the British colonies. The British defeated the French and their Indian allies. A peace treaty in 1763 ended the war, when Canada and most French possessions east of the Mississippi River were given to the English.

Farmers

Many Indiana Indians, ancient and modern, have farming ways! Even pre-contact Indians tilled and irrigated, raising many important crops. Corn, cotton, beans, squash, melons, sunflowers, gourds, pumpkins and tobacco are all native Indian crops!

First on the Land

Archaeologists believe early human beings pushed in to the Great Lakes region sometime after the last great ice sheet retreated northwest, about 10,000 years ago. The first Indianans were wandering bands of hunters. Around 7000 B.C., pine and birch forests sprang up. The early people began to make tools, jewelry and other objects from local materials.

Fire Drill

A device used by Indians to make fires which consisted of a stick and a piece of wood with a tight hole in it. The stick was twirled rapidly in the hole, creating friction that would ignite shredded grass or wood powder placed nearby to start a fire.

Fort Wayne

Built by American General "Mad" Anthony Wayne at the confluence of the St. Marys and St. Joseph Rivers. A crude wilderness fort, it was built over the site of a former Miami Indian tribe village. The location later became one of Indiana's largest cities.

Fur Trade

Began when Europeans came, eager to grow rich from the animal pelts. Trading had a huge impact on the Indian. To get the newcomers' goods, Indians worked as trappers for the French. A flintlock gun cost 12 beaver pelts. The ultimate cost was much more expensive — the loss of the Indian's way of life. Many Indians gave up their traditional farming for trapping and came to depend on the Europeans for the necessities of life.

G is for . . .

Godfroy, Francis

Half French and half Indian. Became a Miami chief and led the tribe in its last war party. Opened a trading post near the town of Peru and became rich.

Games

Adults played ball and other games of chance or skill. Indian children spun tops, fought pretend battles, did target-shooting, walked on stilts, played hide and seek, or competed to see who could hold their breath the longest!

Gorgets

Beautiful ornaments hung around the neck or from ears; their significance, if any, is unknown.

Gens

Group of related members from different tribes.

Gathering

Native Americans gathered natural materials for food, fuel, baskets, clothing, and housing. American Indians tribes also hunted to meet basic needs. Even though some tribes planted crops, most did some kind of gathering.

Gourds

Hollowed-out shell of a gourd plant's dried fruit which often grew into a specific shape. Indians raised many species of gourds. They were used for spoons, bowls, masks, rattles, and even storage.

Golden Garbage!

Archaeologists have uncovered ancient garbage heaps made of animal bones and big piles of clam shells in Indiana. This trash full of treasures has helped them understand the early native inhabitants of our state better.

H is for . . .

Hair

Indians used hair as a textile. Hair from bison, mountain sheep, elk, moose, deer, dog, rabbit, beaver, or even humans were used to weave cloth, make wigs, or stuff pillows, balls, dolls or drumsticks.

Hatchet

A small, short-handled ax, primarily used as a tool, not as a weapon. When settlers moved in, stone hatchets were replaced with iron ones.

Horn and Hooves

Indians used animal horn to make spoons and dishes. Hooves were made into rattles and bird beaks were used for decoration.

Hopewell Culture

Early people who lived in the Ohio Valley from about 100 B.C. to A.D. 500. Anthropologists believe they had a layered society with a defined organization and code of conduct. Because of this, they could work together to build great earthenworks called mounds. They also had an extensive trade network from the Midwest to the eastern U. S. seacoast.

Hunters

Early Indian peoples were hunters who used wooden spears with stone points to kill many kinds of large mammals that are extinct today, such as mammoths and mastodons!

Horses

Spaniards brought the horse to America. At first, Indians were afraid of the horse or thought it was sacred. Later, Indians "broke" horses gently, often "hypnotizing" them with a blanket. Horses were used for transportation, trade, barter or payment. Some Indians ate horse meat in hopes of gaining the animal's power.

Huntington

City laid out in 1832 at the heart of the once-powerful Miami Nation. Here you can see the Chief Richardville House and Miami Treaty Grounds.

I is for . . .

Indian Awareness Center

Fulton County Historical Society, Rochester. Potawatomi and Miami Indians with roots in Indiana and others are members. Created the Trail of Death Regional Historic Trail with markers from Indiana to Kansas, commemorating the forced removal in 1838 of the Potawatomi.

Indiana

Means "Land of the Indians."

Indian Removal Act of 1830

This federal act gave President Andrew Jackson the power to relocate tribes east of the Mississippi to an "Indian Territory." The forced removal of the southeast Indians later became known as the "Trail of Tears."

Indian Wars

Fighting in the eastern part of the U.S., prompted by fur trading, disrupted the Indians in our state and caused settled tribes to begin to move. The Miamis and their relatives, the Weas, Potawatomis, Kickapoos, and Piankashaws had just recently come to Indiana in the early 1700s. The Delawares, Munsees and Shawnees lived on the Atlantic seaboard until bloody wars drove them into our state. Everything was in such constant transition, that most Indian tribes stayed only 25-50 years in our area before moving westward.

Independence

Native American tribes are sovereign nations. That means they are independent. Some even issue their own passports! However, Native Americans are also considered citizens of the United States and enjoy all the rights and privileges of U.S. citizens.

Indian

In 1493, Christopher Columbus called the native people he met in North America "Indians" because he mistakenly believed he had sailed to India! Today, this term includes the aborigines of North and South America.

Indian Ladder

Indians made ladders by trimming branches off a tree. Some were left at consistent intervals to provide steps.

Indian Tribes in Indiana

At one time or another, these tribes have lived in the state of Indiana:

Kickapoo, Lenni Lenape, Mahican, Miami, Potawatomi, Shawnee, Wyandot

J is for . . .

Just So You Know . . .

Today you can find many Indiana Indians that follow some traditional ways. But there are also many who are entrepreneurs, doctors, lawyers, educators and even politicians! If you visit a reservation or cultural event, make sure you know visitor etiquette. Often dances are religious ceremonies and should be observed as such; religious dances should not be applauded. Photography, videotaping and drawing are all important issues - check with the tribe or individual before any is started.

Jesuits

Roman Catholic priests called Jesuits were among the first to meet and live with the North American Indians. Their writings, sent back to Europe, serve as one of today's best references to early Indian life.

Justice?

For hundreds of years, Native Americans have not received justice from federal and state governments. Native Americans have had nearly all their land taken away. Native Americans still have to fight for their rights in courts across the land.

Judicial Termination

Modern term to describe current efforts by various U.S. government agencies and officials (especially the judicial system) to legally decrease the sovereignty of independent Indian tribes.

Just In Time!

The Indian Arts and Crafts Act of 1990 makes it against the law to pretend that an item has been made by Native Americans if it is really not. It is illegal to offer or display for sale, or sell any art or craft product in a way that falsely suggests it is Indian produced.

Jerked Meat

Thin strips of buffalo, elk, deer or other animal meat which is dried on racks in the sun; also called "jerky."

K is for . . .

Kinkash

1832 band of Potawatomi Indians that lived on the Tippecanoe River.

Kokomo

Miami village named after their chief. The name means "young grandmother." Today the site of the Indiana city of the same name.

Killed Pottery

Pottery placed in a grave as an offering to the dead person was called killed pottery. A hole was formed in its base during creation. Often broken pottery was placed in a grave because Indians believed the spirit of the dead person would then be released and could travel.

Knife

Made from various materials such as bone, reed, stone, wood, antler, shell, metal, or animal teeth (bear, beaver, etc.), knives were used as weapons but also creative handiwork.

Kickapoo

Algonquian Indian tribe that once roamed today's Wisconsin, migrated and split. A band of them settled along the border of Indiana and Illinois, at the Wabash River. Allied with the Sauk and Fox from early history. Some fought in the Black Hawk War of 1832.

Knots

Tied on bowstrings, spearhead and arrowhead lashings, snowshoes, and other items, knots were sometimes used to keep track of the days like a calendar—each knot equaled 1 day.

L is for . . .

Linguistic Families

There are 56 related groups of American Indian languages. A few of these speech families include Iroquoian, Algonquian, Siouan, Muskogean, Athapascan, and Wakashan.

Leggings

Both men and women wore cloth or skin covering, which were often decorated with quills, beads, or painted designs, for their legs.

Lost Tribes of Israel

This historic theory has been floating around since 721 BC. The 10 lost tribes of Israel are supposedly groups of people gathered together by Sargon, the King of Assyria. Some say he cast out 10 of the 12 tribes of Israel. Many have tried to prove that the American Indians are these missing tribes!

Lenni Lenape

What the Delaware Indians called themselves; means "real men." Forced to give up lands many times. Lived in at least 10 different states and signed 45 different treaties, often believing they were leasing the land.

Little Turtle

Miami chief. Born near today's Fort Wayne. Had an excellent military mind. In battle, combined tactics used by white generals with the Indians' ability to fight in the wilderness. In 1790, lured an army led by Gen. Josiah Harmar into the Maumee River Valley, which he defeated with a surprise attack. In the next year, he defeated Gen. Arthur St. Clair's army near today's Portland. With 600 of 2,000 men killed, this was the largest defeat of the U.S. Army by the American Indian. In 1797, visited Washington, D.C. Met a Polish general who gave him a pair of pistols and had his portrait painted by Gilbert Stuart, the famous artist who painted George Washington's portrait.

Land Loss

Native Americans lost their land in many ways. Conflicts with other tribes, colonization, European settlement, treaties, and removal took away Indian lands.

Lance

Spear used for hunting and war. The hunting lance had a short shaft and a broad, heavy head. The war lance was light and had a long shaft.

Lariat

These throw ropes made of rawhide, buffalo hair, or horsehair sometimes measured up to 20 feet long!

M is for . . .

Maize

Also called Indian Corn. Known as a "cereal" plant because it probably began as some form of grass. The Indians in our state figured out every possible way to use corn as a food. The only thing the white man added was the creation of "corn flakes!"

Miami Indians

Tribe who established the most permanent roots in Indiana. Lived here around 150 years, in central and northern Indiana. Their territory extended from the middle Wabash River to what today is the city of Fort Wayne. Formed a crucial alliance with the Shawnee. They called themselves Twightwees, a name that came from the cry of the crane. Lived in villages where they grew corn, beans and pumpkins. Houses were made of poles stuck in the ground covered with bark or cattail mats. Patches of deerskin carefully sewn together were their clothes. The villages were filled with music and dance during festivals. They played instruments: drums made of animal skins and rattles made of gourds. They were very religious, believing in an all-powerful creator, other lesser gods, life after death and good and evil spirits that lived in the forests, rivers and even inside of rocks! By 1827, they had sold all their lands and moved to Kansas.

Mahican

This tribe originally lived in upstate New York. The Mohawk dispersed the tribe in 1664, sending one group east and another west. A portion of the western group moved to Indiana and merged with other tribes, including the Lenni Lenape.

Moccasins

Indian shoes made of animal skin.

Mounds State Park

Near Anderson on the White River. Site of 10 ancient earthworks built by Woodland Indians more than 2,000 years ago. The largest is 360 feet around!

Mound Builders

About 2,000 years ago a wave of migrating people came to our area. They were the first of many groups to be known as the Mound Builders, for the earthenworks they created. Sometimes built high earthen walls around their villages, possibly for defense. They vanished long before the first white explorers reached Indiana.

N is for . . .

Nomadic

A way of life in which people frequently moved from one location to another in search of food. "Seminomadic" people had permanent villages, but left them in certain seasons to hunt, fish, or gather wild plant foods.

Neconga

Miami village once located in Indiana.

Nation

There are many Indian nations located within the United States, such as the Miami Nation. Indian nations are called nations because their governments and laws are independent of and separate from the U.S. government. The federal government must have "government to government" relations with these Indian nations, just as it would with foreign nations, like England or Spain.

November

In 1990, President George Bush approved a joint resolution designating November 1990 "National American Indian Heritage Month." Similar proclamations have been issued each year since 1994.

Names

Indian names were often changed during one's lifetime. These names could be derived from events that happened during the person's birth, childhood, adolescence, war service, or retirement from active tribal life. Some names came from dreams, some were inherited, and sometimes names were stolen or taken in revenge. Today some Indians maintain old, traditional Indian names, while others take modern names. Since settlers often did not read or write Indian languages, they recorded Indian names phonetically (as they "sounded"). Thus Indian names were often misspelled.

National Museum of the American Indian

The Smithsonian's National Museum of the American Indian on the National Mall in Washington, D.C., symbolizes a deeper understanding between America's first citizens and those who have come to make these shores their home.

Northwest Ordinance

With its passage, guaranteeing freedom of religion and other rights to settlers, frontier farmers stormed Indiana, which seemed like an invasion to the Indians!

O is for . . .

Osceola, Indiana

Named after the great Seminole chief.

Old Bones

No one knows for sure when the first people came to North America, but scientists have dated bones and artifacts discovered at Clovis, New Mexico around 11,200 years old. Testing on a skeleton found on the Channel Islands, off the coast of California showed they were about 13,000 years old. And, evidence of human habitation in southern New Mexico suggests that people may have been there as far back as 38,000 years ago.

Oil

Indians extracted oil from the many layers of fat that came with fresh bear meat. The fat was boiled down in earthen pots to produce the oil, which was stored in gourds and pots. The oil was used for cooking and even beautifying the body! Indians would mix red pigment with the oil, add the fragrances of cinnamon and sassafras, and rub it all over their bodies.

Origins

Some scientists believe that Native Americans actually came across a land bridge between Asia and North America. They say that during an ice age thousands of years ago, the water level was much lower and people could have walked between the two continents.

Ouiatenon Fort

(Say wee-AUGHT-e-non) One of the forts that the Indians managed to claim during the French and Indian War. Built by the French on the Wabash-Maumee water highway. From 1717-60, was a thriving fur-trading post with a population of almost 2,000.

Orators

Many Indian leaders were excellent public speakers. Powerful and dramatic speakers were vital to leaders who wanted to influence their tribe. Watch for famous Indian quotations in literature and textbooks!

Office of Indian Education Programs

This is a service organization devoted to providing quality education opportunities for American Indian people. Established in the latter part of the nineteenth century to carry out the federal government's education commitment to Indian tribes, it has become the only national education system for American Indian children and adults.

P is for . . .

Powwow

The original form of the word meant "medicine man." Medicine men would often use noise motion and confusion to scare away harmful spirits and cure people. It was also a gathering to talk about political matters. Today, the powwow is an event where Indians gather to sing, perform ceremonial dances, and share cultural pride and traditions.

Potawatomi

The most advanced farmers of the Three Fires Council. Burned away grass and brush to clear fields for planting. Principal crops were corn, beans, squash and tobacco. After the harvest, they moved their villages into the forests to be protected from the winter winds.

Pokagon, Simon

Chief of the Potawatomi Indians. Born in 1830. At the age of 14, was sent to school at Notre Dame in Indiana. Spoke many languages and was probably the most educated Indian of his day. Wrote many magazine articles and a book, printed on birch bark. Managed tribal affairs for 43 years, even helping collect a $150,000 claim from the Government. Died in 1899.

Pemmican

Indian food made of animal meat, which was dried in the sun, pounded together with fat and berries. The mixture was packed into skin bags and used primarily while on the trail.

Paint

Indians used many natural materials to make paint, like clay mixed with oil or grease. Yellow "paint" was made with the gall bladder of a buffalo! Why did they paint their faces or bodies? Indians used paint to look scary or beautiful, to disguise themselves, or to protect their skin from sunburn or insect bites. Indians often applied red paint because it symbolized strength and success.

Pottery

Indian pottery was made from built-up spirals of clay that were molded or paddled, or a combination of the two methods. Most pottery served as cooking vessels.

Papoose

An American Indian infant aged between birth and one year is called a papoose. A papoose spent most of his or her days snugly wrapped in a kind of cradle made of skins or bark and a wooden frame that hung on the mother's back. This sturdy frame also allowed a mother to lean her papoose against a tree or rock within sight as she worked.

Peshewah

Former Miami Indian chief. Born near Fort Wayne around 1761. Also called John B. Richardville. Became very wealthy. Russiaville (a combination of his Indian and French name) is named for him. Died in 1841.

Q is for . . .

Quillwork

Indians used the quills of porcupine or birds to make a type of embroidery. Quills were dyed with juice from berries and other materials. When they were ready to be used, the quills were either mashed with teeth or softened with hot water and flattened with rocks. The quills were then laced into moccasins, shirts, pipe covers, and other items. Beads which Indians received by trading with settlers eventually replaced quillwork.

Quality

Native American arts and crafts are known for their excellent craftsmanship and striking designs. This work is often influenced by things found in nature especially plants and animals.

Quiver

Case used to hold arrows; made of woven plant materials or animal skins.

Quarry Site

A location where Indians went for workable stone such as flint and made stone tools.

Quirt

A short riding whip with a wood, bone, or horn handle.

R is for . . .

Rain Dancing

The rain dance ceremony, performed to encourage rainfall, was common among Indian religions because good weather is vital for a successful harvest. Rainmakers were in tune with nature; there are actual reported cases of Indians producing or preventing rain!

Roots

Indians used plant roots for food, medicine, dye, baskets, cloth, rope, salt, flavoring, and just to chew!

Rattles

Indians of Indiana made rattles from bird beaks, animal hooves, bones, pods, seashells, turtle shells and other animal parts. The rattles are used in ceremonies.

Russiaville, Indiana

Named for an Indian called Peshewah.

Rawhide

Untanned animal hide. The "green" hide was stretched on the ground or over a frame. Flesh and fat were removed. The skin was dried, washed, then buried with wood ashes which made the hair come off. Used by the Indiana Indian to make drumheads, lash lodge poles, mend broken objects and in many other ways.

Reservations

The U.S. government set aside, or "reserved," land for the Indians. These reservations originally served as a sort of prison during the beginning stages of Indian removal. At that time, reservations provided the government with some control over Indian activity and residency. This land was usually considerably less desirable land than the Indians' native territories. Today's reservations are lands that are tribally held, yet protected by the government.

Removal

The U.S. government policy of the 1830s-1850s that removed Indians from their native lands to new lands, primarily west of the Mississippi River.

S is for . . .

Sign Language

A way for Indians to communicate with others from a tribe whose language they did not speak.

Shaman

Medicine man and spiritual leader who was supposed to have special healing power from another world.

Sonotabac Prehistoric Indian Mound and Museum

Vincennes. Largest ceremonial mound in Indiana; exhibits from 10,000 B.C. to the present.

Sweatlodge

Structure used for ritual purification by sweating from exposure to very hot fires or hot steam from pouring water over hot stones. Also called a sweathouse, for some tribes also doubling as clubhouses.

Shawnee

Indians who migrated north from Kentucky and North Carolina. They split into different groups and migrated often. Introduced cultural traits of the southern tribes to the northern tribes, and vice versa. Had villages along rivers in southern Indiana at one time.

Stone-boiling

Cooking method by placing preheated stones into cooking vessels.

Sacred Bundles

A group of objects treasured by a tribe. They were well-guarded and often taken into battle. The items were publicly shown only on very important occasions.

Saddle

While some Indians did use saddles on their horses, most rode bareback!

Spemicalaba

Shawnee; also known as High Horn. Taken prisoner as a child by General Logan, who raised him and gave him the name of James Logan. Became a captain and fought with the Americans in the War of 1812. Died in 1812 of wounds sustained in battle.

Signals

Indian signs made with a pony, blanket, mirror, smoke, fire-arrow or other item to communicate over long distances.

Sachem

The supreme Indian ruler of an area where there are many related tribes.

T is for . . .

Tobacco
A sacred plant early Indians used to make offering to their gods, cure diseases, bring good luck, seal agreements and bind treaties.

Treaties
Written agreements between the U. S. government and the Indians, most of which involved the Indians giving up their native lands.

Tippecanoe
Miami Indian name for an Indiana river. Names means "buffalo-fish place." Also the name of a village on the Wabash River which was once occupied by the Miami, then the Shawnee.

Topeah
Son-in-law of Miami chief Richardville. Also known as Francis laFontaine. Became chief and primary negotiator when the last of the Miami were relocated to Kansas in 1846.

Toisa
Former Potawatomi village near today's Bloomingsburg in Fulton County.

Three Fires
The Potawatomi, Chippewa and Ottawa formed a council by this name. They all spoke Algonquian dialects and shared a common cultural tradition, but otherwise had different economies and day-to-day living habits.

Tracking
To follow a trail by finding a sign such as a broken blade of grass, a moved stone or moccasin track. Indians learned to trail as children, so that they could find food, track enemies and disguise their own signs.

Tacumwah
Miami matriarch and mother of Chief Richardville.

Tenskwatawa
Brother of Shawnee chief Tecumseh. They both founded a religious community on the banks of the Tippecanoe River near today's Lafayette. When Gen. William Henry Harrison, governor of the newly-formed Indiana Territory, feared Indian rebellion, he gathered an army and marched toward the village. The Prophet told the warriors that the gods would make them invisible to the soldiers and that the bullets shot from their guns would be as soft as rainwater!

Tribe
A group of Indians with shared culture, history, original territory, ancestry, social organization, and governmental structure. A tribe may contain several bands of Indians.

Tecumseh
Shawnee chief. Passionate speaker and tireless political organizer. Persuaded the Great Lakes Indians to set aside tribal jealousies and unite against the white enemy.

U is for . . .

U.S. Bureau of Indian Affairs

Provides public services such as law enforcement, land records, economic development, and education to Indians. Known for mismanagement and ethical problems.

U.S. Army

Many Native Americans have fought bravely for the United States Army. Many have also given their lives for a country that was not always accepting of them.

Unique

Each and every tribe has its own unique customs, language, and traditions.

U.S. Indian Schools

The Bureau of Indian Affairs operates hundreds of federal schools around the nation. Enrollment of Native American children measures in the thousands!

U.S. Indian Reorganization Act

Passed by Congress in 1934, the act authorized Indian tribes to establish and conduct their own governments, and to form businesses.

U.S. Colonists

Called Long Knives or Big Knives by early Indians, who also called English explorers "Coat Men."

U.S. President

Once called Great White Father by Indians.

U.S. Indian Wars

The U.S. War Department has compiled an official list of "Indian Wars" that occurred in the United States. Over 50 wars were fought between the U.S. and the Indians during the period of 1790-1850.

V is for . . .

Vermillion

Kickapoo band that lived on the Wabash River.

Village Councils

These were held in the town (council) house and occurred to discuss and decide important matters. Harmony and agreement was essential to tribal unity. Rather than vote on issues, they were discussed until everyone was satisfied. Anyone who wanted to could speak freely. Everyone did not always agree on the outcome, but everyone avoided conflict by pushing their case.

Vegetable Dyes

Indians could not buy color from the store like we can today. Instead, they created many different colors from the things they found on earth like plants, flowers, shrubs, trees, roots, and berries. They made beautiful and unique reds, oranges, yellows, greens, browns, and violets. These dyes were used for baskets, pottery, weaving, body makeup, and clothing.

Village du Puant

Former Winnebago village located in Tippecanoe County and abandoned around 1819.

Villages

Many Indiana Indians lived in villages! Villages were formed around different clans or bands within the tribe, but could also contain different clans living together. Villages were usually permanent settlements, although semi-nomadic tribes have been known to migrate between permanent villages.

Village of Mota

Potawatomi village near Atwood.

W is for . . .

War Bonnet

Special headdress worn into battle, often adorned with feathers.

Wea

Indians located across from Fort Ouiatenon. A Miami band. Served as middlemen in the fur-trading network between the French and tribes on the prairies to the west.

Wabash

What La Salle called some Indian tribes he met in Indiana around 1682. Name means "bright," which referred to the limestone bottom of the river.

War Dance

Indian braves danced this before going into battle. The dance was a way of assembling the braves and getting them to commit to the fight ahead.

Wampum

Algonquian word for "white." This described beads or strings of beads made of clam or whelk shells. They were used in trade between the Indians and settlers. In 1640, counterfeit wampum was made!

West

After their defeat at the Battle of Tippecanoe, the Indians had little resistance against the whites. They were forced to flee west, leaving behind their burial mounds and the lands that had long been their home.

Whistle

Indians from Indiana made them from the wing bones of birds. The whistles made the sound of the bird the bones came from! Used to communicate, signal, sound an alarm or even flirt with a maiden!

Wyandot

Name of the former Huron Indians that eventually settled in Indiana.

White Man

Indians generally called them Pale Face, a name the white men themselves suggested!

Wild Rice

A lakeshore crop and one of the chief foods of the Indian of the North Central states, especially the Algonquian tribes of the Great Lakes.

XYZ are for . . .

Xenophobe

A xenophobe is someone who is afraid of foreign people, their customs and cultures, or foreign things. Many of the first European settlers were afraid of Native American cultures.

You Bet!

Some Native Americans say that Casinos make a lot of money. Others say that too many people have a gambling problem. In the 1980s and 1990s, many tribes discussed whether or not gambling casinos should be allowed. Now that many casinos have been built across the country, the debate has switched to how it should be controlled.

Zounds!

Between 1871 and 1913, at least 98 traditional agreements between tribes and the United States were negotiated and 96 of them were ratified by Congress. Each agreement remains as law (unless changed by a later agreement)!

ZZZZZZ...

Shamans and medicine men were not the only people who had access to the spirit world. Indians believed that people could make contact with spirits every night in their dreams! Dreamers could travel back to the time of man's creation or far ahead into their own futures. They also believed that dreams contained warnings or commands from the spirits. Many tribes felt that they had to act out their dreams as soon as they awoke. If an Indian dreamed about bathing, for example, he would run to his neighbors' houses first thing in the morning, and his neighbors would throw kettles full of cold water over him.

Y... Or, "Why?"

1. Why do you think Indian warriors carried charms with them? Some Indian medicines have been scientifically proven to have true healing power and are still used today. Do you think their charms had any real power to help them win battles?
2. Why do you think the American government kept relocating Indians onto reservations and then making the reservations smaller and smaller?
3. Why did Indians use items such as a pipe in ceremonies? What kinds of symbolic objects do we use in ceremonies today?
4. Why and how did Indians use natural materials in creative ways?
5. Many Indian tribes are running successful businesses on their reservations today. There is one industry that many tribes are making a lot of money at. Do you know what this is? Hint: "I'll bet you do!"

Which Famous Native American Am I?

Solve the puzzle!

Word Bank

Black Elk	Crazy Horse	Sitting Bull	Sequoia
Sacajawea	Chief Joseph	Geronimo	Pocahontas

Down

1. This Shoshone woman joined Lewis and Clark as their guide and translator and helped make the expedition a success! Hint: She has 4 "a"s in her name!
4. This man gave the Cherokee their first alphabet so that they could write. Until then, they communicated only by speaking and drawing pictures. Hint: A famous ancient tree also has the same name!
5. He was one of the fiercest of Indian warriors! He fought against white settlers in Arizona and New Mexico to keep his people from being pushed off their lands. Hint: Jump!

Across

2. A legend says that this brave Algonquian woman saved the life of Englishman John Smith. Hint: Disney produced a movie about her.
3. He fought at Little Bighorn when he was only 13! He was also a wise "shaman" who saw visions and could advise people. Hint: Part of his name is an animal with antlers!
6. He was a great Sioux warrior who won the battle against General Custer at Little Bighorn in 1876. Hint: His horse was not crazy!
7. A leader of the Lakota (Sioux) tribe who lived on the Standing Rock Reservation in North Dakota after the battle of Little Bighorn. He tried to make conditions better for his people there, so the U.S. government called him a "troublemaker." Hint: He did not sit all the time!
8. A wise and brave chief of the Nez Percé who tried to bring his people to Canada to escape war. He said, "From where the sun now stands, I will fight no more forever." Hint: His father's name was "Old Joseph."

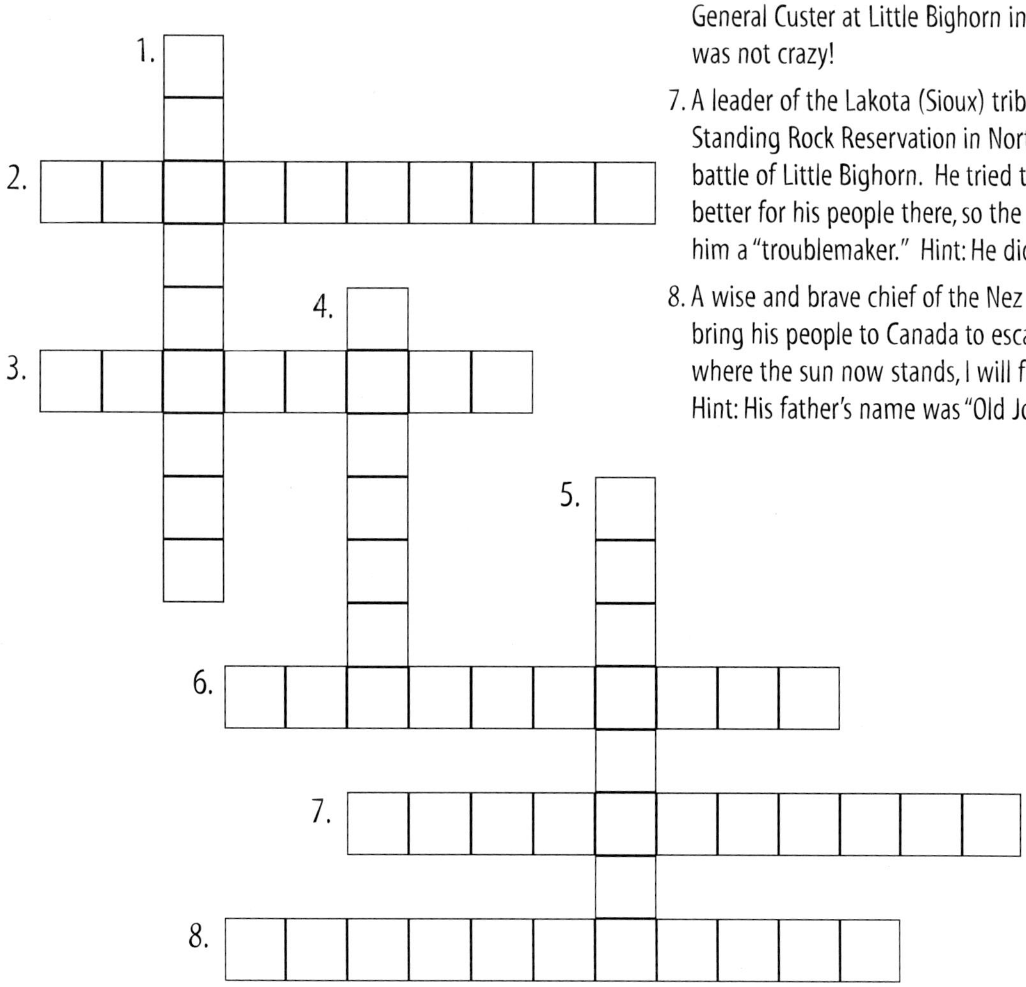

Answer Key: 1. Sacajawea; 2. Pocahontas; 3. Black Elk; 4. Sequoia; 5. Geronimo; 6. Crazy Horse; 7. Sitting Bull; 8. Chief Joseph

Different Ways for Different Indians!

North American Indian tribes are divided into different areas. In each of these areas, tribes shared common ways of living with each other. They might make similar arts or crafts, they might eat the same foods, or they might have had the same beliefs. These activities are all part of their "culture." Each area had its own culture, which was different from the tribes in all the other areas.

Below is a map of all the different groups of Indian tribes in North America. Color each area with a different color. You will see a colorful picture of how Native Americans can all be called "Indians" but still have very different cultures!

Celebration!

Powwows are big festivals where Native Americans gather to sing, dance, and eat together. It is a time to celebrate and show pride in their culture. Powwows can last from one afternoon to several days. The Indians dress in native costumes and dance ancient dances to the beating of drums.

Artists sell their arts and crafts. You might be able to buy some real Native American food cooked on an open fire. Native Americans go to powwows to be with each other, share ideas, and just have fun! Most powwows are also open to people who are not Indian. It's a great place to learn about Native American culture!

If you went to a powwow this weekend, what do you think you would see? What do you think might NOT be there? Circle the objects you think you would see at a powwow. Put an X through those you probably won't see.

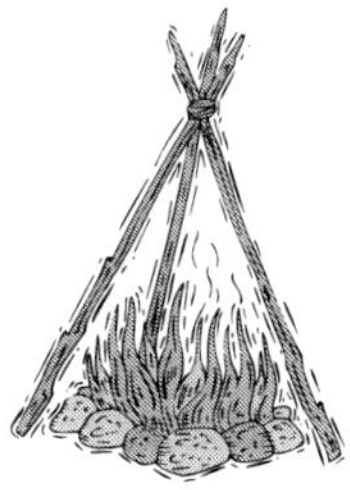

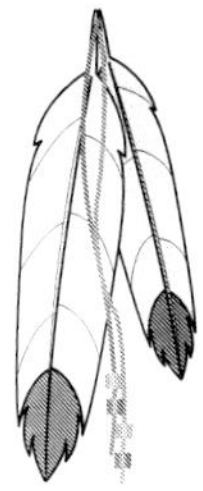

Answer Key: Circled objects are: beads, moccasins, open fire, drums, feathers, baskets, kids, food, drums, horse.

Make an Indian Weaving!

Many Native Americans used weaving to create useful things like sashes (belts), bags, mats, and blankets. They used animal hair to make yarn, and dyed the yarn with natural dyes from fruits and other plants. They also used some plant fibers, like cotton, to make weaving thread.

Weave a small Native American mat of your own. Use different colors of yarn to create a beautiful pattern in your weaving. Place a favorite object on the mat or hang it on your wall!

Prepare the "loom"

Cut a piece of cardboard 5 inches wide and 6 inches long. Along the two 5-inch sides (the "short" sides), have an adult cut slits 1/4 inch deep. These slits should be 1/2 inch apart from each other. So, on each short side you will have 9 slits.

Directions:

1. Take a long piece of yarn and bring it from the back through the first slit (the one next to the edge of the cardboard.) The end of the yarn will hang down behind the cardboard.

2. Bring the yarn right across the front of the cardboard to the slit opposite the one your yarn came through.

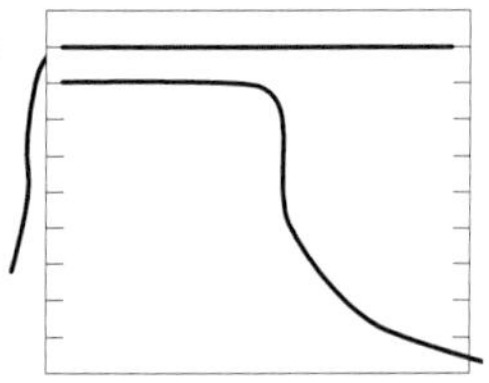

3. Now bring the yarn under the back of the cardboard and then up again through the second slit.

4. Repeat #2 and #3, until you have 9 strands of yarn across the front of your cardboard!

5. Then cut the yarn and tie the two loose ends in the back of the cardboard.

6. Take another piece of yarn and start feeding it through the 9 strands, going over one, under the next over the next, etc. When you get to the end, pull the yarn behind the cardboard and around to the front, and begin again. This time, whatever strand you went over, go under. And whatever strand you went under, go over.

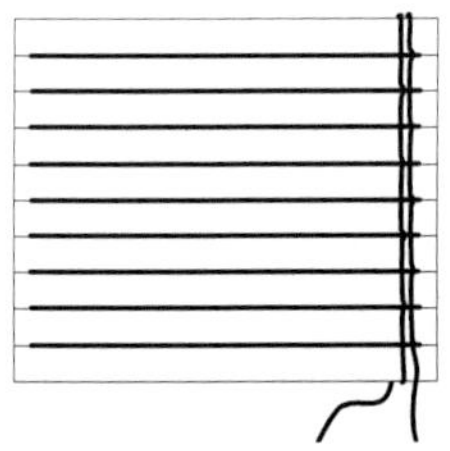

7. Repeat this pattern until the front of your cardboard in covered. Then cut the yarn in the back of the cardboard, and trim it to create a fringe for your mat!

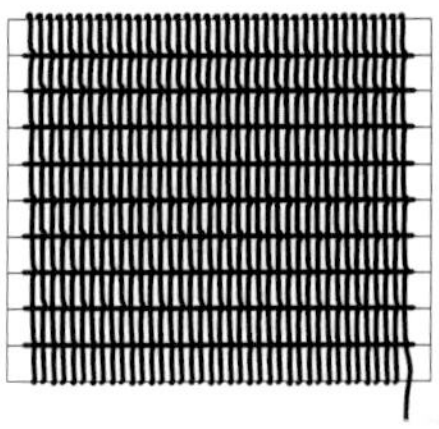

Tips:

- For a wild look, use variegated or different colored yarn!
- For a tighter mat, push the under/over strands up against the previous strands during weaving.
- To keep your mat from unravelling, tie neighboring fringe together up close to the mat.

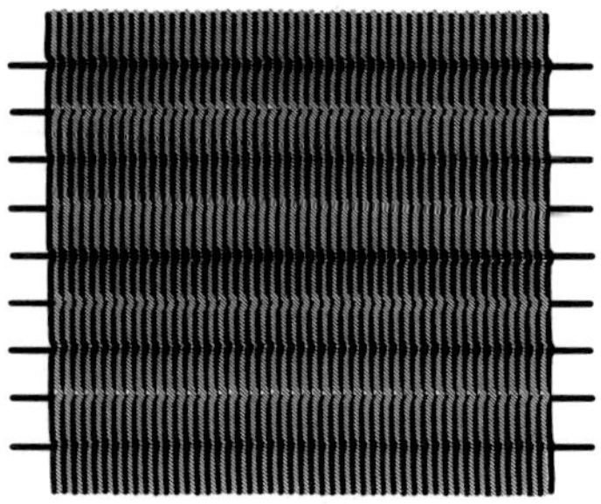

Finders Keepers?

Native Americans have many buried treasures. For hundreds of years, special objects would sometimes be buried with Native Americans, or maybe they would just be lost. Archeologists used to dig for interesting artifacts in old Native American gravesites. They would keep the Native American bones or the arrowheads, rattles, masks and other objects that they found. But this made the Native Americans feel like they were being robbed.

In 1990, the U.S. government passed a law that said that no one could look for or take these Native American objects anymore. And whoever had any already had to give them back to the people they belonged to. This is called repatriation

Help the archeologist return the artifact to a Native American.

Fast Fact

An artifact is an object that was made by people a long time ago for some useful purpose.

Busy Hands!

Before modern times, Native Americans didn't have stores where they went to buy things. They made everything they needed.

What did Indians make with their own hands? Use the Word Bank and pictures to find out!

Word Bank

blanket	moccasins	arrows	pottery	canoe
mat	food	jewelry	pouch	box

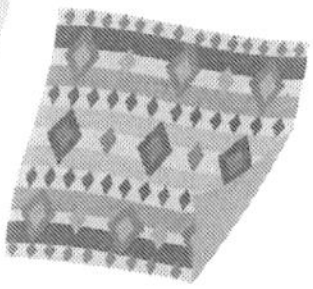 ___ ___ ___

 ___ ___ ___ ___

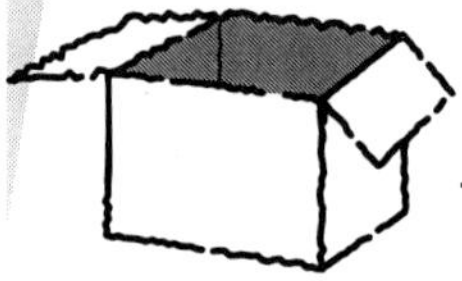 ___ ___ ___

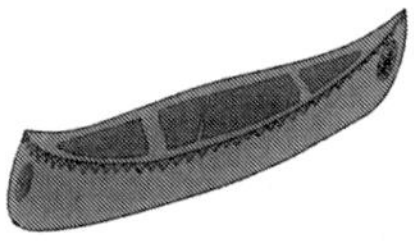 ___ ___ ___ ___ ___

 ___ ___ ___ ___ ___ ___ ___

 ___ ___ ___ ___ ___

 ___ ___ ___ ___ ___ ___ ___ ___ ___ ___

 ___ ___ ___ ___ ___ ___

 ___ ___ ___ ___ ___ ___ ___

 ___ ___ ___ ___ ___ ___ ___

American Indians Today

Beginning with the first letter of each group of letters, cross out every other letter to discover some new words. You may not have heard of these before, but you can read all about them!

1. Many Indians live on these, but many more do not!

TRYELSDEBRNVJAOTPIPOWNASX

____

2. Many Indians have been poor for a long time because for many years the government took away their lands and their ability to make a living.

TPKOOVWEBRNTXYA

____

3. Many Indians have been studying hard at school and going to college in order to earn more money. Education helps the Indians make their lives better. These Native Americans are working to become:

TSJUMCBCFEYSMSOFPUVL

____

4. This is a big term that means Native Americans have worked hard to get the U.S. government to let them rule themselves. This means that they have their own laws and make their own decisions. They are like a separate country inside the U.S.! Now, try and see if you can get your parents to give you the same thing!

TSGENLBF **JDGEETSEWRAMCIHNUAKTYIKOTNU**

______________ ______________________________

Fast Fact

What do Indians work as today?

- doctors
- nurses
- factory workers
- artists
- lawyers
- actors

The same kinds of jobs any American might work at!

Native Americans Move to the City!

Solve the code to discover the mystery words!

A	B	C	D	E	F	G	H	I	J	K	L	M
✷	❀	⌘	♣	➧	❤	❢	✬	✂	✆	☛	✈	✉
N	**O**	**P**	**Q**	**R**	**S**	**T**	**U**	**V**	**W**	**X**	**Y**	**Z**
✿	☆	❖	✡	✏	❥	☎	✒	✙	✖	✍	✠	✓

1. During the 1950s and 1960s, the American government paid Indians to leave their homes on reservations and move to cities to get jobs. If cities are sometimes called urban areas, then these brave Indians were called:

✒ ✏ ❀ ✷ ✿   ✂ ✿ ♣ ✂ ✷ ✿ ❥

2. Many Indians chose to stay on their reservations and not move to the city. They thought that if they moved to the city, they would lose the way of life that their parents and ancestors had taught. These Indians called themselves:

✏ ➧ ❥ ➧ ✏ ✙ ✷ ☎ ✂ ☆ ✿   ✂ ✿ ♣ ✂ ✷ ✿ ❥

3. Native Americans who moved to cities lived close to each other. They tried to keep their way of life as much as possible. They did not want to forget their religion, native art, or music. They did not want to lose their:

⌘ ✒ ✈ ☎ ✒ ✏ ➧

4. Are you afraid of heights? Many people are. The Mohawk Indians are not! Many of them work hundreds of feet above the city to build steel frames for skyscrapers. People who do this work above the city are:

❥ ☎ ➧ ➧ ✈   ✖ ☆ ✏ ☛ ➧ ✏ ❥

5. Today urban Indians and reservation Indians come together to celebrate their culture. They share ideas and stories. They dance and beat drums. They make and sell Indian jewelry. During these celebrations, Indians remember how much they have to be proud of! These big parties are called

❖ ☆ ✖ ✖ ☆ ✖ ❥